Car
Smarts

Sheela Chari

Children's Press®
A Division of Scholastic Inc.
New York / Toronto / London / Auckland / Sydney
Mexico City / New Delhi / Hong Kong
Danbury, Connecticut

Special thanks to Wright Honda, Drexel Hill, PA

Book Design: Michael DeLisio
Contributing Editor: Matthew Pitt
Photo Credits: All photos by Maura B. McConnell, except p. 16 © James Marshall/Corbis

Library of Congress Cataloging-in-Publication Data

Chari, Sheela.
Car smarts / by Sheela Chari.
    p. cm. -- (Smarts)
Summary: Offers advice for young drivers on the different factors to consider when deciding to buy or lease a car.
ISBN 0-516-23927-9 (lib. bdg.) -- ISBN 0-516-24012-9 (pbk.)

1. Automobiles--Purchasing--Juvenile literature. [1. Automobiles--Purchasing.] I. Title. II. Series.
TL162 .C4254 2002
629.222'029'7--dc21

                                   2002001902

Contents

Introduction 5

1 Driving the Dream 9

2 Purchasing Tips 13

3 Lease the Wheels 27

4 Easy Rider 33

New Words 42

For Further Reading 44

Resources 46

Index 47

About the Author 48

You're in the backseat of your parents' car when you see it out of the window: your dream car. It's a convertible with tinted windows. It's painted your favorite color, a deep blue. The only problem is, you're not in the driver's seat. As the midday sun gleams off the hood, the car appears to sparkle like a diamond. You get so distracted, you don't hear your parents when they ask you what's wrong: "Why do you look so excited?" You're too embarrassed to say. Just yesterday you saw an ad for that car on TV. You'll never have that kind of money, though! Besides, the announcer started talking about needing $4,000 down, leasing plans with an option to buy, an introductory APR of zero percent...blah, blah, blah. He might as well have been speaking in another language. What does all that stuff mean? Before you know it, the light

Once you turn sixteen, it's easy to start dreaming of the day you'll get behind the driving wheel.

turns green. The blue car takes off down the boulevard, like a dream you forget the moment you wake up. Does owning a car like this have to be just a dream? Not necessarily.

These days, more young people are driving cars than ever before. Having a car means freedom, but it means taking on responsibility, too. To own a car, you need to save enough money, and learn how to take care of your car once you get it. This is sometimes easier said than done. Teens usually have small incomes and aren't old enough to get a loan from a bank by themselves.

With some time and effort, however, owning a car can become a reality. The search for your dream car can be done mostly on the Internet. By using a computer at home, school, or the library, you can get the information you need. Even if you don't have Web access, there are plenty of magazines, newspapers, and organizations to assist you. This book is a great place to start!

Part of the fun of choosing a car is going on test drives. These experiences often help you decide which cars might be right for you.

Chapter 1

Driving the Dream

Many teenagers start thinking about owning a car before they even get their driver's license. However, age is not the only way to tell if you're ready for your own car.

BE RESPONSIBLE

Cars are a big responsibility. Car-related accidents are the main cause of death in teenagers between the ages of sixteen and twenty. As a young driver, you should focus on learning good driving habits from the start. This means paying attention to the road, not the radio. Always look out for your safety, as well as the safety of your passengers.

While driving can be fun, it's also a very serious responsibility. If you take your eyes off the road for even a moment, you are taking a dangerous risk.

Being responsible off the road will help prepare you for being careful on the road. Holding a job, getting good grades, and taking care of duties at home all show signs of being responsible.

MANAGE YOUR MONEY

Purchasing and maintaining a car is very costly. Sometimes parents or guardians might buy a car for their child. Or they may expect their child to help out with monthly payments. They may also ask that their child pay for expenses, such as gas, oil changes, insurance charges, and maintenance.

Money Matters

If you're planning to pay for some of the expenses, you may need to get an after-school job. Restaurants, department stores, and libraries are good starting places to look for jobs. Ask neighbors and friends to keep their eyes open for employers who need extra help. Check the newspaper classifieds for openings, too.

Once you get a job, open a checking or savings account at a bank. If you are under eighteen, your parents will need to open an account you could use. A good rule of thumb is to save at least 10 percent of each paycheck or your monthly allowance. Keep track of what you spend and save. At any time, you should know roughly how much money is in your account.

HAVE A PLAN

Before you purchase a car, there are many things to consider. How long do you plan to keep it? If you only want the car for a couple years, think about buying a used car, or leasing one (see chapter 3). If you plan to drive often or for long distances, you should explore a different option. Find a car that gets good gas mileage, and can handle heavy usage and changes in weather. It's best to purchase a car that fits your individual needs, even if it means spending a little more money, or passing up on the car of your dreams. Be realistic about your plans and expectations.

Fast Fact

The price of more affordable new cars starts around $12,000.

Chapter 2

Purchasing Tips

Once you've worked out financial issues with your parents, and once they feel you're ready, it may be time to buy a car. Do you know where to begin? Here are some tips to keep in mind.

BUYING NEW

The advantage to buying a new car is that all the parts come under warranty. A standard bumper-to-bumper warranty means that anything that breaks down in your car will be fixed, at the dealer's expense. These warranties usually cover a specific timespan and a certain amount of mileage. A three-year, 30,000-mile warranty would expire three years after you had purchased the car, or after you

Each time you meet with a car dealer, be sure to bring plenty of questions to the table.

had driven 30,000 miles—whichever comes first. New cars have the latest safety features, such as dual-side airbags. You know you're getting the latest technology.

One big disadvantage is that new cars cost more. If you're on a small budget, you may need to choose one of the low-end cars, which are small and lighter. In an accident, these cars are less safe than larger, heavier cars. Also, low-end cars depreciate quickly. This means that their value goes down fast. A car that you buy for $10,000 may only resell for $8,000 a year later.

BUYING USED

Considering a used car is a smart idea. Used cars may be cheaper than new cars. However, many times you will get a much better car for your money, with a better resell value. Also, the insurance rates on used cars are often less.

The disadvantage to buying used is that you don't always know what you're getting. Without

Although this used car might be inexpensive, the repair costs could get pretty steep.

that factory warranty, a used car may end up costing you more overall. Frequent repair bills can really put a dent in your wallet.

VEHICLE TYPE

If your whole family will be sharing the car, then four-door sedans, station wagons, or minivans are good choices. These cars are big, safe, and offer

With so many automobiles to choose from, you'll need lots of patience while shopping for the right one.

maximum storage space. Sports utility vehicles (SUVs) are also popular family cars. However, SUVs get poor gas mileage. If you get one, you'll be making frequent, and costly, trips to the gas station.

If you'll be the main driver, a two-door sedan is another, sometimes cheaper, option. Many two-door sedans have a hatchback instead of a trunk. This feature provides you with more storage space.

FIGURE OUT A BUDGET

There are four types of expenses you might have when you buy a car: the down payment, the monthly installments, the insurance, and the maintenance.

Down Payment and Monthly Installments

A down payment is what you agree to pay right away for the car, at the moment you sign the contract. You must borrow the rest from a bank. You'll be expected to pay back this loan in monthly installments, along with interest. The larger the down payment, the less your monthly payment. Most loans must be paid back within twenty-four to sixty months. If you borrow from a bank, a parent or guardian may have to co-sign the loan.

Insurance

Car insurance is used to pay for accidents. There are different kinds of automobile insurance. Everyone, however, is required by law to have liability insurance.

If there is an accident, liability insurance pays for injuries you cause to other people and their property. Another type, collision insurance, pays for damages to your car.

To get insurance, you must pay a premium, or fee, every month. The premium is determined by many factors. These factors include your driving record, age, where you live, and the kind of car you own. There are ways you can lower your premium. Owning a car with top-notch safety features and having a superb driving record will help. Taking a defensive-driving class and getting good grades in school could also keep your costs down. Speak with a good insurance agent to find out what types of insurance are best for you. The agent will also be able to tell you how much your insurance will cost.

Maintenance

The first scheduled maintenance for a new car usually comes after six months, or after driving 6,000 to 7,500 miles. Important scheduled maintenances also occur at 30,000, 60,000, and 90,000 miles.

Try to ask experienced mechanics to explain the inner workings of your automobile. It's always a good idea to know what makes your car run.

Reading material like the Kelley Blue Book *and* Consumer Reports *will keep you in the know on the latest automobile information.*

Even though your new car's warranty covers any needed parts and labor, there is a set cost for maintenance service. The costs for each servicing aren't the same. The first servicing is the cheapest. The 60,000-mile servicing is the most expensive because the largest number of parts gets inspected and replaced.

You'll need to take your used car into the shop for regular performance checkups, too. Taking great care of a used vehicle will lengthen its life on the road, and keep you safe and sound behind the wheel.

DO YOUR HOMEWORK

Web sites like *edmunds.com* and *autoweb.com* provide important information about prices for each type of car. This includes the manufacturer's suggested retail price (MSRP), the invoice price, and the car's true market value (TMV). The MSRP is the price set by the car manufacturer. The invoice price is the lowest number of the three. It's the price the dealer has to pay the manufacturer for the right to sell the car. The TMV is the "going," or current, price for the car. The TMV is what you might expect to pay.

However, the closer you pay to invoice price, the better the deal is for you. If the car is used, you can look up its make, model, and year to see how much it's worth. Magazines like *Consumer Reports* and *Road & Track* are also valuable sources of performance and pricing information. *Consumer Reports* even has a fee-based service that will provide you with information by fax or E-mail.

TEST-DRIVE

Always make appointments to test-drive a car that interests you. Do this whether you're buying a new or used car from a dealer, or a used car from an individual. By doing this, you'll rule out finding any unpleasant surprises after you've bought the car. Test-drive at least two or three different cars, in city traffic as well as on the highway. If the car is used, check that its features—such as the heater and radio—are in working order.

BEFORE YOU BUY

When you've found a car you like, here is a checklist of things to do before you negotiate:
- If someone is co-signing a loan for you, get your application preapproved by the bank.
- Know how much it will cost to insure your car.
- Make printouts of your car price from popular car Web sites or magazines.
- Know the TMV for your car.

A dealer may tell you that the car you've got your eye on is a winner. By test-driving the car, though, you'll be able to put those claims to the test.

If you're buying a used car, here are a few more steps:

- Know the "blue book" price for your used car. This price is listed in the *Kelley Blue Book.*
- Get a copy of all maintenance records from the car owner.
- Have a mechanic inspect the car.
- Write down the car's make, model, Vehicle Identification Number (VIN), and gas mileage.
- Run a detailed car history report on the Web.

Negotiations for a new or used car can sometimes get pretty heated. Just remember that you're holding the most powerful tool: the words "No thanks."

NEGOTIATION

There's no getting around it: Negotiating can be tough. It is often the most nerve-racking part of the process. However, if you know exactly how much you are willing to pay, you can be firm about your offer. If you're buying a new car, describe to the dealer all the options you want, such as air conditioning or power locks, before you start negotiations. Always use your printouts as a starting point. If you're negotiating for a used car, use the *Kelley Blue Book* price instead. Make your starting offer lower than the TMV or blue book price. By the end of negotiations, you should agree on a price that's close to what you want to pay. If the price is much higher than the TMV or the blue book price, find another place to buy your car.

Definitely feel free to bring your parents along to the negotiation process. You may want to rehearse with your parents before speaking with the dealer. Remember: The dealer is not talking with you to make a friend—only to make a profit. Don't let the dealer pressure you, and be wary of ploys. Above all, make sure your questions are being answered clearly. If you have doubts, or feel the dealer is being unfair, don't be afraid to leave. Dealers' personalities can differ greatly. If the first one you meet makes you uncomfortable, walk away with no regrets and try someone else.

In 1985, a new car company called Saturn was founded. Saturn created a "no-hassle, no-haggle" policy. They offer one standard price (the MSRP), are up-front with it, and do not negotiate. This is designed to take the pressure off both the dealer and the buyer.

Chapter 3

Lease the Wheels

There is another option to car ownership besides buying. This option is known as leasing. These days, one out of every three vehicles is leased. Every year, leasing gets even more popular.

So, what does it mean to lease? Basically, it means that you agree (in a written contract) to pay for using a car for a specific period of time. Most leases are between two and four years. Some offer you an option to buy the vehicle at the end of the lease. However, many experts agree that buying at the end of the lease is not a good idea. You'd be better off buying a new car, or a used car in excellent condition. When leasing, you agree to make payments on the first day of each month, until your lease expires. You pay insurance and keep the car in good working order, as you would with any car you buy.

Leasing a car is a fairly complex thing to do. However, if you do your homework before you meet the dealer, you'll be ready for the challenge.

At the end of your lease, you give the car back to the dealer. If the car has no more than normal wear and tear, your commitment is over. If you haven't taken good care of the car, you will be charged to have it fixed.

Haggling

Some dealers may try to tell you that, with a lease, you must pay the car's full sticker price. Don't be fooled. Leasing also leaves room to negotiate. Even many adults don't know this. Experts estimate that 85 percent of people who buy or lease a car don't do any homework before seeing the dealer. Don't make this same mistake.

The Price of Freedom

The amount of your monthly lease payment depends on the car's depreciation charge. You pay the difference between the car's original worth and what it will be worth when your lease ends. The box on page 29 provides examples of depreciation by comparing a sedan with a subcompact.

Original Value (sedan) $20,000

Depreciation (after two-year lease) $15,000

You pay the difference of ....$5,000 (plus finance charges)

Original Value (subcompact) $13,000

Depreciation (after two-year lease) $7,000

You pay the difference of ....$6,000 (plus finance charges)

In this case, it would actually cost you less to lease the more-expensive sedan. That's because it depreciates less quickly than the subcompact. This is one of the bonuses with leasing. It can actually be a better deal to lease a higher-end car than a lower-end one.

Monthly payments are less for a leased car than a new car. However, once the lease ends, you must

Be sure the length of your lease is exactly equal to the manufacturer's warranty. If your lease and the warranty are both for three years, the manufacturer covers any problems with the car. However, if you have a three-year warranty, and a four-year lease, any repairs during that fourth year come out of your pocket.

Don't be afraid to ask to see the fine print of any contract before signing it.

return the car. Of course, you can lease again and again, but you'll continue making payments every month. If you buy a new car, you'll eventually make your final payment. Then you'll own that car. It will be yours to keep or sell. A lease can put you in a more luxurious car for a shorter period. Either way, you need your parents to act as cosigners. Dealers will only grant lease contracts to people with an extremely good credit history. Unfortunately, teenagers aren't old enough to have created a good credit history.

Upsides to Leasing	Downsides to Leasing
• Lower monthly payments	• You must keep the car for the entire lease period
• Getting a new car every two to four years	• Giving up the car when the lease ends
• Low (or no) maintenance costs	• Paying a penalty if the car is returned with high wear and tear
• No down payment required	• Customizing the car (repainting, adding a CD player) is not allowed

Chapter 4

Easy Rider

Learning From Others

Now that we've learned some basics of buying a car, let's find out how someone else did.

MARIA

Maria, a sixteen-year-old, just got a job at a department store 7 miles from home. She decides to buy a car so she can get to work. She already has $3,800 saved. She'll have to ask her parents to help her borrow the rest. Before she talks to them, she tries to learn as much as she can about buying a car.

Finding the Right Car

Maria's family doesn't have a computer, so doing Internet research at home is not an option.

If you have access to the World Wide Web, you're in great luck! You'll be able to learn about any vehicle on the information superhighway.

Maria doesn't get discouraged. She simply goes to the local branch of her library after school lets out. She reads the *Kelley Blue Book*. She also reads copies of *Consumer Reports* magazine. The librarian notices what Maria is researching, and informs her that Internet stations are available at the library. Maria looks on the Internet to find a car she can afford. She finally decides on the Griffin. This car has an MSRP of $13,205 and an invoice price of $12,421. *Edmunds.com* reports that the TMV is $12,490. She likes the Griffin because it has strong safety features, gets good gas mileage, and is roomy inside.

The Griffin seems like a good, low-end car that is perfect for the type of driving she will do. She also sees an ad for last year's model of the car in the classifieds of her local newspaper. The car is only one year old, and the owner is asking for $10,000. Maria is concerned about buying a used car, though. She is worried that it won't run well. Maria decides not to call the owner, and to go with the newer model instead.

Adding the Expenses

Maria figures out her monthly car payments by using a loan calculator on the Web. Her monthly payment comes out to $172. Next, she calls her family's car insurance company. She finds out that a new Griffin will make her family's premium go up $100 each month. After the call, Maria makes a chart.

Monthly Income		Monthly Costs	
Job:	$315.00	Car payment:	$172.00
Allowance:	$ 50.00	Insurance:	$100.00
Baby-sitting:	$ 65.00	Maintenance:	$100.00
Total:	$430.00	Total:	$372.00

From her chart, she sees that she will have about $58 left over each month to call her own. Although she's used to spending more money, Maria thinks she can make the change. Now she's ready to talk to her parents.

Negotiating With Parents

Maria's parents think her idea to buy a new car is a good one. They'll help out, but only if she signs a contract. The contract asks her to drive only under safe conditions and to use good judgment while driving. After a long discussion, Maria agrees. A copy of the contract is pictured on page 37.

Once the contract is signed, Maria's mother agrees to co-sign a loan. Their application for a loan is approved by their bank.

Test-driving

Maria makes appointments to test-drive some cars. She looks at the Griffin, as well as a few other competing models. Maria likes how the Griffin handles on the freeway. The car feels roomy, yet it's small enough that Maria is comfortable making sharp turns and merging into traffic.

CONTRACT

Having a driver's license and driving a car are privileges. All privileges have to be earned. This means that driving privileges can be taken away by either parent when any of these rules are broken:

1. Breaking the driving laws or abusing a car can mean losing your driving privileges, even if we learn about it from someone other than the police. You never know who may be watching you.

2. You will maintain your grades, conduct, and attitude at the same high level as when we granted you driving privileges.

3. No one else should be allowed to drive a car entrusted to you. This means that you may not lend your car to friends.

4. If you are ever in a condition that might make you less than 100% competent behind the wheel of a car, phone us to come and get you. You will not lose your driving privileges.

5. You should never be a passenger in a car in which the driver is not 100% competent to drive. A call to come and get you will not mean that you will lose your driving privileges.

6. If you can't reach us, hire a taxi. We will pay for it.

Margarette Lopez
Signed by Parent

Maria Lopez
Signed by Teen

Because Maria did her research and stayed relaxed, she was able to strike a great bargain.

Negotiating With the Dealer

Maria decides to buy her car from the dealer closest to her house. This way, she won't have far to go for service checks. She's nervous about talking to the sales agent. However, she's done her research and has printouts of prices from different Web sites. To her surprise, Maria's negotiation with the dealer doesn't last long. This is because the dealer knows the Web sites that Maria has seen, too. When Maria shows her printouts, the dealer has to give a price that's very close. After about 15 minutes, they agree on $12,400. Maria is happy, since it's close to the *edmunds.com* suggested price. She and her mother sign the papers. Maria has purchased her first new car.

How Did Maria Do?

Maria did a great job investigating new cars. She probably could have dug a bit deeper with her used car search. Maria's friend Ron, who was also looking for a Griffin, saw the same classified ad that Maria read. He got the car's VIN number and did a lemon check, or a record report. Ron then bought a thirty-day, unlimited auto-history report on the Web. This report told him that the used car was in great condition and had no problems. Ron got his used Griffin for $9,900. Ron got a slightly older car, but he also paid $2,500 less.

Still, Maria did her homework, and wound up with the car she wanted. In figuring out her budget, she also remembered to call the insurance agent to get an estimate, and to include maintenance as another expense. She might have found a better deal if she had negotiated with several dealers, not just the one closest to home. To help lower the monthly premium for the car insurance, Maria should plan on taking a defensive-driving class.

Conclusion

As you now know, it pays to do your homework. Let books, magazines, and the Internet make your job easier. Using these resources, collect as many facts as you can. Know what you can afford and the kind of car you really need. Always include insurance, maintenance, and repair as a part of your future expenses. If you're buying a used car, *always* run a full vehicle history report, using one of the Web sites listed at the back of this book. Lastly, it's *very important* to have a reputable mechanic do a thorough inspection of any used car you're thinking of buying. An inspection costs between $50 to $150. Don't be afraid to pay this price. It could save you headaches, and thousands of dollars, down the line.

Heads Up

Every year, thousands of wrecked cars are fixed and sold again under new titles. An on-line car history report is the best way to keep yourself from ending up with one of these wrecks. Be sure to get a full, detailed report, even if it costs extra money. Don't trust a free lemon check or other free record reports to give you all the information you need.

collision/comprehensive insurance
insurance used to pay for fixing your car
after an accident

co-sign to sign a contract or document jointly,
agreeing to share financial responsibility

deductible the money you have to pay when
you're in an accident, before your insurance
will pay for the rest

depreciation when the worth of something
goes down after it is used

designated driver a person who doesn't
drink alcohol so he or she can drive
friends home

down payment money that you agree to pay
right away toward a purchase

interest if you're borrowing money, the extra
fee you must pay to repay the money you've
borrowed; if you're saving money, the extra
amount the bank pays you for keeping your
money with them

invoice price the price the dealer pays the manufacturer for a car

lemon a junk car

liability insurance insurance used to pay for injuries you cause to other people and their property in an accident

manufacturer's suggested retail price (MSRP) the price the manufacturer sets for a car

preapproved loan a sum that a bank promises to lend

premium the fee you must pay every month for car insurance

re-titled a car that has been fixed up and sold again under a new title

true market value (TMV) the current price, or what you can expect to pay for the car

vehicle identification number (VIN) no two cars have the same VIN

For Further Reading

BUYING GUIDES (published annually)

Consumer Reports. *Consumer Reports New Car Buying Guide.* Yonkers, NY: Consumer Reports Books.

Consumer Reports. *Consumer Reports Used Car Buying Guide.* Yonkers, NY: Consumer Reports Books.

Kelley Blue Book. *Kelley Blue Book Used Car Guide.* Irvine, CA: Kelley Blue Book.

Van Sickle, David, ed. *AAA New Car and Truck Buying Guide.* Yonkers, NY: American Automobile Association.

For Further Reading

CAR MAINTENANCE

Jackson, Mary. *Car Smarts: An Easy-to-Use Guide to Understanding Your Car & Communicating with Your Mechanic.* Emeryville, CA: Avalon Travel Publishing, 1998.

Sclar, Deanna. *Auto Repair for Dummies.* Saint Paul, MN: Hungry Minds Press, 1999.

Web Sites
PRICING INFORMATION

These sites provide accurate, up-to-the-minute information on car prices. The Autoweb and Edmunds sites even have links to loan calculators.

Autobytel
www.autobytel.com
Autoweb
www.autoweb.com
Cars Direct
www.carsdirect.com
Edmunds
www.edmunds.com

LEMON CHECK SITES

CarFax: Vehicle History Reports
www.carfax.com

Auto Check
www.autocheck.com

Index

B
blue book price,
   23, 25

C
collision insurance, 18
contract, 17, 27, 31, 36
co-sign, 17, 22
credit history, 31

D
dealer, 13, 21-22,
   25, 31, 38, 40
depreciation, 28
down payment, 17

I
insurance, 17-18,
   27, 40
interest, 17
invoice price, 21, 34

L
lemon check, 39
liability insurance,
   17-18

M
maintenance, 10,
   17-18, 39-40
monthly installment,
   17
MSRP, 21, 34

N
negotiating, 24-25

P
premium, 18, 35, 40

R
resell value, 14

New Words

T

TMV, 21–22, 25, 34

V

VIN, 23, 39

W

warranty, 13,15, 20

About the Author

Sheela Ramaprian Chari holds a Master of Fine Arts degree in Creative Writing and works as a technical writer at IBM. Part of her job is explaining how things work to other people. She feels that learning about car ownership can teach young people how to be independent and take care of themselves in the future.